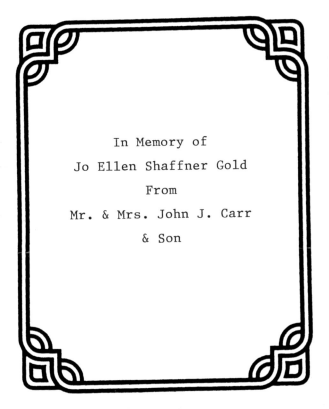

In Memory of
Jo Ellen Shaffner Gold
From
Mr. & Mrs. John J. Carr
& Son

The DARING
COAST GUARD RESCUE of the
PENDLETON CREW

THERESA MITCHELL BARBO AND
CAPTAIN W. RUSSELL WEBSTER (RET.)

Illustrations by JULIA MARSHALL

Charleston   London

THE
History
PRESS

J
BAR

Published by The History Press
Charleston, SC 29403
www.historypress.net

Copyright © 2013 by Theresa Mitchell Barbo and
Captain W. Russell Webster
All rights reserved

First published 2013

Manufactured in Canada

ISBN 978.1.62619.095.5

Library of Congress CIP data applied for.

Dedicated to our Friends, the Gold Lifesaving Medal Crew of the CG 36500

BM1 Bernard C. Webber
EN3 Andrew Fitzgerald
SN Ervin Maske
SN Richard Livesey

On Whose Shoulders Today's Rescuers Stand

We also dedicate this work to

Master Chief John E. "Jack" Downey
(USCG Ret.)

*Our colleague on the 36500 Leadership
Lecture Series*

CONTENTS

CHAPTER 1

JACK'S SNOWY MORNING

On February 18, 1952, ten-year-old Jack Nickerson of Chatham awoke to a flurry of white snow outside his bedroom window.

He sat up and peeked outside the frosty window, his hand holding the blue checked curtain to the side for a better view. Fresh snow the color of flour clung to the sides of his house. Bits of snow had crept beneath many of the gray-brown shingles. The scene reminded Jack of his father using a hammer and nails to hang a large picture on the wall for his mother. That's the way the snow looked—like a pretty picture on the side of their clapboard and shingle house.

Even the other windows were dotted with a fresh thin layer of white. The heat from inside the home melted a neat circle in each windowpane. No dirt in the yard was visible because every inch was covered. From the tops of bushes next to the pantry window, the snowfall measured at least a foot.

Jack thought his house looked like a penny postcard, like the ones sold at the Ben Franklin General Store on Main Street that the tourists from Boston buy every summer.

And to Jack's delight, the storm was hardly over. Snow continued to fall and snowflakes hung in the air, silent and beautiful.

Jack wiped the sleep from his hazel eyes. He shifted his attention from the window next to his bed to the floor. In the doggie bed was Sinbad, a big yellow dog. Sinbad lazily opened one eye and wagged his tail twice at Jack. Sinbad had been Jack's companion since he was five years old. They went everywhere together, except, of course, to Jack's school.

Sinbad was named for the famous Coast Guard mascot of the same name that a ship's crew adopted in 1938. There was even a book about the first Sinbad published a few years ago. Jack had a copy in his bookcase.

"Morning, Sinbad," Jack said cheerily. "How are ya, boy?" Jack stretched his arms and yawned. He brushed aside the brown hair that had fallen onto his forehead as Sinbad yawned and fell back asleep, his large head snuggled against a plaid cushion.

Jack lay back down and pulled his bed sheet, a red wool blanket and three homemade quilts up to his chin. Jack especially loved the red blanket because his granny had sewn his initials into the border: JEN, for John Eldredge Nickerson.

Last night, Jack had complained there were too many blankets on his bed. But when she tucked him in, Granny Lucille Eldredge, his mother's mother, suggested that by morning he would be grateful for the extra warmth.

"You weren't born when the 'five-quilt' winter of 1905 nearly froze us to death on Cape Cod," she said.

Granny was right. Jack was glad for the extra layers. The temperature was far below freezing, and the extra blankets had kept him toasty. Granny had even brought in an extra blanket from the work shed for Sinbad's bed.

In fact, it was Granny who had given Sinbad to Jack five years before. Jack and Sinbad had grown up together. They were bonded like two peas in a pod. At least that's what everyone said.

Jack tried to sleep for a few more minutes. He burrowed into the covers to keep warm. But Jack couldn't close his eyes again.

He had too much on his mind.

Jack figured school was cancelled because his mother, Mary, had not awoken him earlier either to eat or do chores. That meant he had the day to himself!

His young mind suddenly raced with possibility, as fast as the Old Colony Railroad on its way from Chatham to Orleans. Maybe he would tag along with his dad on errands to town. Or hang out with his best friend, George Sears, a neighbor. George had the coolest train set. It was made by Lionel. Together the boys had spent many hours together playing with the set. George had received it from Santa last year.

If they didn't play with trains, he and George might take Sinbad sledding at Chatham Bars Inn. That is, if he could avoid shoveling the front and back walks at the house.

George's and Jack's mothers were cousins. And the women were close friends—best friends, in fact. They spent a lot of time together, which meant that Jack and George grew up like brothers. Their mothers, Mary Nickerson and Kathleen Sears, were together often. Sometimes it was just for tea or coffee at the kitchen table. Jack and George would come home from school and find their mothers together, "visiting," as they called it.

In the spring, Mrs. Sears and Mrs. Nickerson helped each other with their gardens. The women shared the small crops of strawberries in June and bright red tomatoes in July. And there were always freshly baked sugar cookies and homemade lemonade for Jack and George and the other boys they hung out with. As families, the Sears and Nickerson clans attended community functions together. They shared Thanksgiving dinner. Jack and George still talked about the plump, juicy drumsticks.

Jack wondered what George was doing now.

Like Jack, George had probably slept in. Jack stretched his arms out wide in bed and looked around his room. He loved his private space. Because their house was fairly roomy,

Jack had his own room. It wasn't a large room, but it was his.

Jack's parents had let him choose the paint color, so he went with a light blue. Jack drove with his father into Orleans to buy the paint from Hinckley's Hardware store. The blue reminded him of the color of the water off the fish pier at noontime in summer.

The navy blue checkered curtains his mother had sewn for him hung from two windows facing south toward Nantucket Sound. He often fell asleep to the sounds of foghorns and clanging ship bells, all music to his ears. The rotating light from the nearby lighthouse crawled across the ceiling of Jack's room, and the sight was mesmerizing and lulled him to sleep every night.

Jack's baseball bat and glove were on a small oak desk in the corner next to his schoolbooks. A small bookcase held his treasure-trove of Lone Ranger books, Marvel comics and a piggybank. Jack put his chore money in the bank. He loved the matinee movies in town, and each film cost twelve cents. The clunky radiator in the corner blasted warmth throughout Jack's small blue bedroom.

Jack had an older brother, Joshua, and a baby sister named Susanna. Well, she really wasn't a baby, but at the age of three, Mother still called Susanna "my baby girl," so the nickname stuck since the child always seemed glued to her mother's hip.

All three Nickerson children had hazel eyes and brown hair. Their mother called them her "little stair steps" because they lined up in size like a staircase going up. Jack knew he was a lucky boy to be in this family.

Hunger was getting the best of Jack.

The smell of oatmeal and bacon wafted up the stairs and seemed to call his name. His stomach was growling through his flannel pajamas.

"John Eldredge Nickerson, time for breakfast!" his mother called. "Get dressed and come downstairs, please."

CHAPTER 2

FAMILY

I n a minute, Mom!" Jack replied, as he began to dress himself and make his bed. His mother always did that—used his full name to call him downstairs only for breakfast or supper, for a chore or when he was in trouble. George's mom did the same thing: "George Taylor Sears, I have an errand for you!" "George Taylor Sears, run this letter to the post office!" Neither Jack nor George minded because they knew their strict mothers loved them a lot.

And Jack and George thought their mothers did this because they were proud that their maiden names were their sons' middle names, a tradition in their closely knit families. It was, after all, a tradition on Cape Cod to use names in this fashion. This tradition had been around for centuries in Chatham.

The smell of his father's favorite black coffee filled the kitchen when Jack came downstairs a few minutes later. He loved spending time with his father, Samuel Atkins Nickerson.

Mr. Nickerson was a fisherman. Jack's grandfather and great-grandfather were also fishermen. It was a dangerous job, and Jack was very proud of his father. Jack didn't think he wanted to be a fisherman, but he knew he had years to think about it. The idea of being a train conductor seemed mighty appealing. But what Jack wanted to do more than anything else in the world was to join the U.S. Coast Guard.

Jack's father fished year-round. In winter, his boat, the *Susannah*, worked the waters just offshore in local fishing grounds. But in summer, Jack's father took the *Susannah* all the way to the Grand Banks for cod. He was gone for up to a week at a time. Samuel had a crew of five, all of whom were very kind to Jack.

Once in a while, Jack would go with his father and his crew on daylong fishing trips. His mother wouldn't allow him any longer at sea than one working day. But when she did allow him to go, she packed a wonderful lunch and put their food and drink in a large wicker basket. Ham sandwiches, pickles, homemade cookies and a jug of either water or cider, depending on the season. Once, Samuel and Jack found half an apple pie wrapped up in a cloth just for them to enjoy.

But it was on the family's sailboat, a schooner named *Heritage*, where Jack had the best time with his dad. Free from work as a fisherman, Samuel was left with nothing to do but enjoy the sea with his first mate, his son Jack. Samuel told Jack many stories about sea adventures. Pirates and storms and lost lands far from shore were among his many tales. And Jack loved all the stories.

Usually Sinbad tagged along, wagging his big yellow tail as the white canvas sails of the *Heritage* left Stage Harbor. Jack loved taking the wheel under his father's watchful eye for a few minutes at a time. He waved to the other boats as they passed by.

Soon Jack became very good at handling boats even though he was just ten. Jack was skilled at rowing the family's small dory boat that was needed to reach the *Heritage* at its mooring.

One boat caught his eye time and time again and actually became part of Jack's dreams: the Coast Guard's *36500*, a thirty-six-foot-long rescue boat. The *36500* was moored a short distance away from the *Heritage*. Jack had seen the *36500* in the waters off Chatham. He longed to be part of the Coast Guard and aboard the motor life boat, even more than he wanted to be a train conductor or fisherman.

One Coast Guardsman in particular was Jack's idol: Bernie Webber. Jack had met Bernie a number of times at the Chatham Pier when Samuel Nickerson's fishing boat was offloading cargo. Samuel and Jack had also seen Bernie on Nantucket while Bernie was on Coast Guard duty there. Bernie had introduced Samuel and Jack to his friend Millie. Millie volunteered for the Coast Guard. She lived on Nantucket. Millie became good friends with Samuel and Jack. In fact, she had given a puppy to Samuel to give to his mother-in-law, Lucille, Granny Eldredge, for company. She and Granny were old friends. But Granny Eldredge wisely thought that Jack should have the puppy, not her.

Millie had explained to Samuel that the puppy's name was Sinbad. He was named after a famous World War II mascot the Coast Guard had adopted. In Jack's arms, Sinbad had finally found a "forever home."

Whenever they met, Bernie had been kind to Jack. He always patted him on the head or slipped a peppermint candy into the palm of his hand. Samuel Nickerson always spoke highly about Bernie. Jack liked that his father and Bernie were friends.

Webber, who was only twenty-four but seemed much older, told Jack stories about rescue missions aboard the *36500*. Bernie's memories became Jack's own memories. Bernie had even given Sinbad a few biscuits every now and then, and the big yellow dog always wagged his tail whenever Webber and his crew were around. And once, Bernie tore off half his Cushman's donut to share it with Jack.

Jack dug into his oatmeal and sprinkled the cooked grain with brown sugar, maple syrup and raisins. He was sure hungry this morning! Susannah was not up yet. Joshua was working his part-time job somewhere in town. It was only Jack, his parents and Granny Lucille Eldredge in the warm kitchen. On a cold morning like this, oatmeal was perfect!

Granny was listening intently to the short-wave radio. Most folks in Chatham had a short-wave to stay connected to happenings on the sea. Chatham was a thriving fishing town in 1952, and most people there had some livelihood connected to the ocean, either as fishermen, fish vendors, sail makers, etc.

They needed to know what was happening to their loved ones offshore. It was a way Granny kept up to date with news on the water about people she cared about: the sons and grandsons of friends who had fishing boats, the comings and goings of people, boats, weather and other news.

And what she was hearing on the radio suddenly alarmed Granny, who had a sharp ear on local news. A big 503-foot-long fuel tanker, the *Fort Mercer*, had broken in half nearby in huge 60-foot waves!

Jack sensed her unease and began to listen too.

Something bad was happening in this storm. But if he was alerted to any news bulletins, he didn't let on to his Granny or parents, who didn't seem to be listening to the short-wave.

Mary Nickerson kept busy washing pots and pans in the sink as she looked out the window at the fresh snow. Samuel was reading the paper, scouring advertisements for new commercial fishing gear.

"Son, I'll take care of shoveling the walks today, don't you worry about it. Go out and have fun," Samuel said.

"Thanks, Dad!"

There was a basket of Cushman's Bakery donuts on the table that Mary had bought from the bread man yesterday. It was an occasional treat that Mrs. Nickerson indulged in for her family.

The donuts reminded Jack of Bernie. Bernie had always said how much he loved Cushman's donuts. How cold Bernie and his crew must be if they were working today, Jack thought to himself between mouthfuls of oatmeal. On a day like today, with the snow and all, Jack thought, surely the *36500* would have to rescue someone.

As he ate, he kept one ear on the short-wave radio where an announcer was talking about the storm.

"Hey Dad," wondered Jack, "where's Joshua?"

"He's out shoveling sidewalks for the town," answered Samuel. "He should be back late this afternoon, son."

"Okay, just wondering," replied Jack.

His thoughts turned to the hours just ahead and what he could do with his day. Jack was ready for a snowy adventure. Any kind of adventure; it was great to miss school!

But the bulletin on the short wave competed for his attention. Several large offshore Coast Guard cutters and Bernie's friend Chief Donald Bangs from Chatham Station were ordered to pick a brave crew and assist the *Fort Mercer*.

As much as a ten-year-old boy could, Jack daydreamed about the hours before him. Jack continued to eat. But something gnawed at him. He knew his friend Bernie would surely be asked to help.

He could sled with George, he thought. Or earn a few pennies shoveling Mrs. Greenough's front stoop next door. Or run errands with his father.

Then the thought came to him.

An amazing, smart idea.

A perfect plan.

Jack put down his spoon.

Of course, why hadn't Jack thought of it *sooner?!*

If Jack planned it well, he could pull it off and help Bernie at the same time. And make his parents proud of him.

A trickle of brown sugar and maple syrup ran down Jack's mouth as his hazel eyes grew wide as his plan took shape.

Jack had thought of a way to become part of Bernie's crew.

A way to help Bernie. And the Coast Guard.

Sinbad should come too, of course

Suddenly his plan seemed perfect.

"Son, are you okay?" asked Samuel, who kept one eye on his son throughout breakfast, suddenly clearly amused as he folded the morning newspaper in half and looked at his middle child.

Usually Jack mowed through a meal like a sailboat leading a regatta on a June day in nearby Pleasant Bay.

"Yeah, um, sure, Dad. Just thinking about my day is all," replied Jack, using a cotton napkin to wipe the brown sugar and syrup from his mouth.

"Honey, aren't you hungry anymore?" Granny Eldredge asked her grandson as she moved her hand across Jack's forehead to smooth his hair across a splash of freckles. For a moment, her attention turned from the radio on the counter to her grandson.

"Well you know me, Granny, I'm just suddenly full!" Granny flashed Jack a knowing smile. With a final pat, Granny's warm hand slid from Jack's forehead.

"John Eldredge Nickerson, finish your breakfast, wash your hands and be off with your day," Mary ordered as she wiped her hands on a towel at the sink. "Don't wander too far from the house or from George's place either if you go there."

"Okay, Mom, promise. I left something upstairs, but as soon as I get it, I'll take off," replied Jack.

Since George lived only three houses away, walking to his home, even in a nor'easter, wasn't a big deal. Jack was, after all, a Chatham boy, born and bred for the rough-and-tumble, wind and water.

Jack took a quick gulp of cold milk, tapped Sinbad on the head and leapt up from the table.

His parents looked at each other, rolling their eyes and smiling.

"Whatever our boy is up to, he sure has a vivid imagination!" Samuel said.

"He takes after you, my love," smirked Mary.

Granny Lucille Eldredge looked at them both but didn't say a word. She suddenly seemed worried but couldn't figure out why. She would later say that "something just didn't feel right about what I was hearing on the radio. This will be a very bad storm!"

After fetching something from his room, Jack took off for the mudroom and started to put on his warmest coat, a wool hat with ear flaps, a scarf, gloves and a leash for Sinbad. He put on his boots, remembering to double-knot the laces. Sometimes when he forgot to tie the laces extra carefully, they came loose. Jack tucked the Cushman's donut into his pocket. He was going to need it later.

Time to put his plan into action.

First, though, he had to visit George or else his family would become suspicious.

CHAPTER 3

BERNIE AND THE NOR'EASTER

There was danger everywhere Bernie Webber looked.

The young Coast Guardsman had awoken to a ripe nor'easter that covered most of New England. A nor'easter is like a hurricane. This kind of storm has very high winds beginning from the east. It is very hazardous. In this storm, a lot of snow had fallen already. It was still snowing. And the temperature was extremely cold.

And the hurricane was hitting Cape Cod hard.

"This is going to be one long day!" Bernie sighed to himself.

People were huddled in their homes, safe from high winds and blowing snow. But a lot of property was damaged, and that damage often causes dangerous conditions. And a storm means that many people on the water could be in trouble. Only the Coast Guard could save them.

They could be fishermen at work or passenger ferries running daily routes between Cape Cod, Nantucket, Martha's Vineyard and mainland communities including Boston and New Bedford.

As a member of the Coast Guard, it was Bernie's duty that day to tow fishing boats back to their moorings. Bernie was twenty-four years old in 1952.

If people needed to be rescued, Bernie would have been called out to help them. But today, he was assigned the task of towing back boats that high winds had ripped from their moorings. Moorings are places just offshore that float. They are attached to chains that hold anchors on the floor of the harbor. Boats are attached to moorings with rope to keep them from floating away. When ropes are used at sea, they are called lines.

Bernie had already towed back dozens of boats. He had grabbed the lines of rope and towed them back to their moorings with a Coast Guard vessel. For this job, Bernie didn't use the *36500* motor lifeboat but a smaller boat the Coast Guard owned. It was called a DUKW, or "duck" for short.

As he worked, Bernie was glad that most of his friends who were fishermen, including Jack's father, Samuel, had taken their boats out of the water during February. Fishermen often took their boats off the water in winter for routine repairs. He had seen Samuel a few days ago, and Sam remarked that he was taking the month off to reorder fishing equipment and supplies in time for spring.

In fact, Bernie imagined that Samuel was in his warm kitchen sipping coffee and reading the paper. Samuel also had the *Heritage* on dry dock. The term "dry dock" meant that the boat was now out of the water and on land for routine repairs or off-season storage. But Samuel kept a dory on shore, and Bernie wondered if his dory was still safely stowed beneath the fish pier.

Bernie also wondered what his young friend Jack was up to today. Bernie hoped Jack was sledding at Chatham Bars Inn or building a snowman in his yard alongside Sinbad, that loveable big yellow dog.

"Geez, that kid sure has a great life," Bernie said aloud.

That day, Bernie worked alongside a few buddies from the Coast Guard. Their names were Melvin Gouthro and Richard Livesey. Bernie, Melvin and Richard worked for many hours outside during the nor'easter. They were freezing cold. In 1952, there was no fleece as there is today. The work clothing worn by Coast Guardsmen did not keep them very warm and became soaked with chilling water.

They were very relieved to return to the Chatham Motor Life Boat Station. Bernie, Melvin and Richard were based at the station. They all loved working for the Coast Guard.

When they returned, all three men concentrated on getting warm. Then they wandered into the galley, which is like a kitchen. There is always a cook on duty. That day so many years ago, a young Coast Guardsman named Ervin Maske was visiting the Chatham Motor Life Boat Station.

Ervin was waiting to hitch a boat ride to his lightship in Nantucket Sound. A lightship is a boat that stays anchored in place to warn other ships of danger. The name of his lightship was the *Stonehorse*. Ervin couldn't get a ride to his lightship until the nor'easter had passed.

To wait out the storm, Ervin volunteered to work in the galley. Ervin made pies and bread for the men who worked at the station.

"I spoil you guys," Ervin said to anyone who would listen. And he was right. "Your food is terrific," the guys told him.

Ervin said hello to Bernie, Melvin and Richard as they entered the galley. He fed them navy bean soup and corn bread.

After he ate, Bernie passed by the radio control room, where the short-wave radio brought in messages from boats at sea. And the short-wave radio allowed the Coast Guard station in Chatham to communicate with boats at sea.

Bernie was cold and exhausted. He had been working out in the nor'easter all morning. He changed his clothes and brought his wet uniform to the laundry room to be cleaned. At least now he had something hot to eat and he could rest.

"Hey, Andy, how are you today, buddy?" Bernie said to Andy Fitzgerald. Andy was twenty-one and the station's junior engineer. As an engineer, it was Andy's job to keep the boats in good running order. "Just fine, Bernie," Andy answered, "and glad to see you finally out of the storm!"

Bernie was very comfortable being in the Coast Guard. He had been in the service for almost six years. He had served his country from a young age. Bernie had joined the Merchant Marines at the age of sixteen and served one year. At the age of seventeen, he joined the Coast Guard. He had already served in the Coast Guard at a lighthouse on Martha's Vineyard.

Bernie and his young wife, Miriam, were renting a house in Chatham. The name of the house was Silver Heels. People in Chatham named their homes for different things and even put nameplates out front. This very day, Bernie was very worried about Miriam. She was sick with the flu.

At any rate, Bernie was a young man and leader whom everyone trusted and had faith in.

As Bernie chatted with Andy, Ervin and Richard in the galley, there was a message over the short-wave radio coming into the station's radio room. It was now in the late afternoon of

February 18, 1952. It was a message bearing terrible news.

Earlier that morning, Coast Guard crews from Boston-area stations had been assisting the *Fort Mercer*. Only Bernie's friend Donald Bangs and his crew from the Chatham Motor Life Boat Station were involved in that rescue.

But word had just come from the short-wave radio that a Coast Guard plane had spotted a *second* oil tanker that had also broken apart in two pieces about five miles off Provincetown. The name of that vessel was the *Pendleton*. There was a chance that people could still be alive on the *Pendleton*'s stern, which is the rear section of a vessel.

Bernie's boss, Donald Cluff, was officer in charge of the Chatham Motor Life Boat Station. Cluff was also called "Chief."

"Webber, get into my office now!" shouted Cluff in his usual gruff manner. Bernie came into Cluff's office. "Chief, what's the matter?" he asked, a bit nervous.

Chief Cluff responded in a voice that clearly marked him as a true southerner.

"Webber, go pick yourself a crew. Y'all got to take the *36500* over the bar and assist that yar ship, ya hear?"

CHAPTER 4

THE STORM

Bernie couldn't believe his ears. He was
very upset. But he didn't want his boss
to see his emotions. Bernie kept a stiff
upper lip, and his mind began focusing on the
mission and his orders.

Bernie was being sent back out into the
storm on a dangerous mission that he might
not survive. With his head bent in worry,
Bernie left Cluff's office and wandered onto
the mess deck. He didn't have a minute
to lose.

Bernie was obeying orders to help the crew
of the *Pendleton*, and he looked around for

a Coast Guard crew to assist him. He didn't have to look far.

"Bernie, I'll go with you," said Ervin, who was taking off his galley apron. "I'll get ready now," he added.

"Ervin, thanks so much!" Bernie said.

"I'll volunteer too," said Richard.

"Livesey, that's great, are you sure?" asked Bernie.

"Sure as you're standing there, my friend," Richard added.

"That makes three of us," said Andy. "I'm going too. You guys are gonna need an engineer in case the diesel engine goes kaput!"

Bernie couldn't believe his luck, both good and bad.

Here he was being ordered back into the storm, not even sure if there were survivors aboard the *Pendleton*, but as luck and fate would have it, he couldn't have asked for a better crew.

"We're with you, Bernie, all the way," Ervin said.

The four put on the warmest emergency cold weather clothing they could find, jumped into the station truck and took off for the Chatham Fish Pier.

Bernie had been aboard the *36500* a few days earlier. He loved the boat as much as any boat he'd ever been on. His mind wandered, and he wondered if anyone had remembered the key to the survivor's compartment, a place where eleven people could be tucked away during a rescue. Bernie had the engine key, but another key was necessary to unlock the cabin where survivors were held. "I guess we'll find out soon enough," Bernie thought to himself.

"Hey guys, we should have taken along some Cushman donuts that the bread man delivered yesterday," Bernie said in an attempt to calm their nerves.

"We'll all have one when we get back to the station," Andy remarked.

"Yea, and I'll bake you guys another pie!" Ervin promised.

When Bernie, Andy, Ervin and Richard arrived at the Chatham Fish Pier, they carried extra lines and other equipment to their dory, got in and rowed toward the *36500*. They did run into someone they knew: a local fisherman named John Stello. John Stello turned to Bernie and said, "You guys better get lost." His meaning was that Bernie and his crew should find somewhere to ride out the storm because there was no way they'd survive it on the water.

Bernie's only response was to ask John Stello to phone his wife, Miriam, to tell her that he would be delayed.

It was then that Bernie noticed that other boats were missing in the storm, swept from shore by high winds.

"Darn, Samuel's dory has vanished," Bernie said. Normally the small boat was tethered to a wooden post near the pier for quick access. "I bet it's lost in the storm somewhere too," he added. Bernie made a mental note to keep an eye out for the small dory. Then again, he also thought there was no way he'd see that dory again, not in this storm.

From the fish pier, Bernie, Andy, Richard and Ervin would row a small dory to where the *36500* was moored. Then they would be off over the Chatham Bar to find the *Pendleton*.

The Chatham Bar was in Chatham Harbor. The "bar" was a dangerous area where parts of the harbor were very shallow and the sand shifted frequently, so no one ever knew which parts were shallow or deeper for boats to pass safely through. This meant that taking a boat "over the bar" was very dangerous because big offshore waves would collide with the shallow sandbars, creating steep walls of water. But Bernie had to risk it.

Little did Bernie realize the surprise that awaited him when he got to the *36500*.

Or the danger that lay ahead for his crew.

CHAPTER 5

A PLAN IN MOTION

When Jack left his house, he went straight to George's, and the best friends spent the day reading their books. For lunch, Mrs. Sears let the boys make their own peanut butter and fluff sandwiches. Because this was a "special snow day," the boys were allowed to have chocolate milk with their meal.

In his ten-year-old mind, Jack loved the way Mrs. Sears allowed Sinbad inside the door. Usually dogs weren't let inside. She even snuck Sinbad some cooked chicken from last night's supper when the boys were having lunch. Sinbad spent the afternoon snoozing on George's bedroom floor while the boys played. Jack didn't breathe a word of his plan to George. George would have told on him wicked fast if the plan didn't go well.

Throughout the day, all Jack could think of was the short-wave radio Granny Lucille was listening to and how Bernie might be leaving to rescue the crew of the *Fort Mercer* and how he wished he could be there to help his friend! But it looked like the bigger offshore Coast Guard ships might handle the *Fort Mercer* rescues by themselves without Bernie's help.

But then, about 3:00 p.m., the radios became even more active as reports came in that a second tanker, this one named the *Pendleton*, was discovered just off Chatham. Jack's plan looked like it was back on again. It now looked like Bernie and his crew might see some real action after all!

Jack hoped he wouldn't be too late to put his plan into action.

About 3:15 p.m., Jack told George he had to get going. "But I thought you were staying for supper," George said. "Our moms worked it out a few hours ago on the phone," he added. George was confused. When their mothers had spoken earlier in the day, Mrs. Nickerson had said it was okay if Jack stayed for the family's nighttime meal. Jack often ate with the Sears family. And now Jack was on his way. He was sorry to see Sinbad leave too.

"Um, I gotta go, George. Sorry! But before I leave, let me help you clean up your room." And Jack began to pick up the toy tin soldiers and put them away in a cardboard box. He also picked up three books, including one about the Lone Ranger, off the floor and stacked them in George's bookcase.

"Hey, if there's no school tomorrow let's do something fun," said George. "Maybe we could go sledding? Or ice skating?"

"Sure, I'll let you know." And with that, Jack was off. George couldn't figure out why, but he was confused that his friend didn't want to stay for supper, especially since his mother was making beef stew, Jack's favorite. He could smell the stew and homemade bread downstairs and couldn't wait to eat. Tonight, George would slather the warm bread with gobs of butter and dip the bread in the gravy.

Turning his mind from food, George picked up a book and began to read about the Wild West and cowboys. Then for a moment his thoughts lingered on his friend. Why, George asked himself, was Jack carrying around his red wool blanket, the one that always stayed on the end of his bed? He never had come to his house with his blanket before. That was kinda weird. George continued to read.

Downstairs in the mudroom at George's house, Jack put on his boots, using a quick single knot this time. Hat, scarf, gloves and coat went on next, and then Jack tucked the red blanket under his arm. He snapped on Sinbad's leash around his collar. "C'mon, boy," Jack said. He was relieved George's mother, Kathleen Sears, was not in the kitchen to question him on why he wasn't staying longer.

Quiet as a mouse, Jack gripped the doorknob, and as slowly as he could, he opened the door and slipped out. It would be another hour before George's mother looked out the mudroom window and saw the vanishing footprints of both Jack and Sinbad covered by fresh snow.

As the afternoon slid into dusk and the feisty nor'easter kept up its rage, Jack and Sinbad approached the Chatham Fish Pier, and Jack was relieved that no one saw him there. It was just after 4:00 p.m.

Keeping a low profile was part of his plan. If anyone saw what Jack was about to do, they would try to stop him for sure. Good, his plan was working so far.

A few of the fishing boats had crawled into Chatham Harbor earlier in the day. Their captains were lucky to have made it back safely. Other boats and their crews were still in harm's way in that storm.

Jack's breath left his body and was swept away by the wind and snow of the nor'easter. Although it wasn't a long walk from George's house to the Chatham Fish Pier, the nor'easter made the usual walk of five minutes an even twenty. "Sinbad, how ya doin' there, boy?" Jack asked. As if on cue, Sinbad looked up at Jack, and the pair kept up their pace until they reached the parking lot of the fish pier.

Perfect, no one was near.

Time to begin his plan.

CHAPTER 6

DANGER!

J ack raced toward the family dory tied to the end of the pier.

Whatever light was left in the day began to retreat into dusk.

"Sinbad, quick, get into the boat," Jack shouted above the sound of the wind. "Jump, Sinbad, jump!"

Like he had done dozens of times, Sinbad scooted back on his hind legs like they were springs and charged forward and up, clearing the side of the small boat with ease. He landed in the bottom, near where the oars were stowed, and turned around and looked up at Jack. Sinbad wagged his tail.

Jack untied the dory from its pole and began to drag the boat toward the water through the sand and snow. He had done this many times before but never in a storm. Just before they hit the water, Jack stopped what he was doing. He picked up the red wool blanket and wrapped up Sinbad. The dog looked like a Christmas present. "This will keep you warm, promise!" Jack said.

Jack hopped in and set the oars in their locks. As his boots found their fittings in the wood trim, Jack noticed one of his bootlaces had come undone. "I'll tie them again soon," he said to himself.

Already very cold, Jack also wondered if he was making a mistake. Would his plan work? Could he help Bernie and the Coast Guard? Was he too late? Winds plucked at the freckles on Jack's face. He tucked in his chin as the dory's oars dug into the first wave. Right or wrong, he was off on his journey.

Breathing heavily and trying his best to row through the swells and waves, Jack accomplished something no ten-year-old boy should ever try: rowing a dory to another boat nearby in a storm.

The *36500* was bobbing up and down with each passing wave. There must have been a few minutes' lull in the storm, because rowing was very difficult but not as bad as Jack had thought. It was as if each wave picked up the dory and moved it closer to the *36500*, almost like magic.

Sinbad, shivering beneath the red wool blanket, lay on the floor of the dory with his head between his paws.

In a few more strokes, Jack would reach the Coast Guard boat.

He was breathing heavily and growing very tired. Jack was hungry, and the nor'easter's chill gnawed at his small body through his layers of wool.

With a firm but small grip, Jack caught a line hanging from the *36500* and with all his might pulled the dory alongside the Coast Guard rescue vessel. A rope is a rope until it hits the deck of a ship or boat; then it becomes a line. As he hung onto the line, Jack closed his eyes and lowered his head as if to rest for a few seconds.

Sinbad whimpered, and Jack opened his eyes. Daylight was leaving the skies very quickly. He had only a minute to scramble

onto the *36500*. Jack urged Sinbad to jump, and he did! Even though the dory was a lot smaller and lower to the waterline than the *36500*, the dory lifted during a wave, and it was then that Sinbad jumped. Jack followed Sinbad, clutching the red wool blanket with one fist and the boat line with the other.

Jack didn't know what to do about the dory, so he left it tied to the *36500*.

By this time, both boy and dog were freezing. The wind that had helped to propel the small dory toward the *36500* and the waves that had lifted the dory to the height of the same boat now made Jack and Sinbad very cold.

Jack prayed that the door to the passenger hold was unlocked. He was now becoming very scared. His courage was about to fail him because of the cold. Jack wanted to be in his parents' home, near Granny, warm in the kitchen. Oh, no, what if the door was locked? Would he and Sinbad freeze to death? Jack thought of his parents, of George, but most of all, Jack thought of Bernie. Bernie would feel so bad if something happened to Jack, his young friend.

A lump grew in Jack's throat, and tears burned in his eyes. "I'm gonna be in so much trouble," thought Jack as he clutched the red blanket, the only item that could keep Jack and Sinbad warm. Jack tried to be a big boy. But he suddenly was unsure of himself. The only thing that kept him going was how proud Bernie would be if Jack's plan worked.

Sinbad was already aboard the *36500*, having scampered up by himself and with a small push from Jack. His eyes didn't leave Jack's, and his tail wagged with anxiety.

Then the unthinkable happened.

Just when Jack threw his first leg over the deck, his boot—the one with the untied lace—caught on a brass cleat. The boot started to slip off and dropped into the dory. Jack was halfway aboard the *36500*, with one foot still in the dory. Then Jack lost his footing.

Jack used two hands to grab the thin band of wood rimming the deck. The blanket fell into the dory, with one corner bobbing in the stormy swell. Then Jack's foot dropped into the sea and he felt a frigid bolt of cold shock his skin.

Jack screamed.

Sinbad howled.

But no one heard them.

CHAPTER 7

A CHILD GOES MISSING

The battered blue Coast Guard pickup truck pulled into the empty lot at the Chatham Fish Pier just before 6:00 p.m. With little time to spare, Andy, Bernie, Richard and Ervin hurried out of the vehicle. They were dressed in their emergency rescue gear: oilskins over cotton clothing. The four walked down the stairs toward the pier. At the pier, a smaller boat was located to bring them to the *36500*, which was on a mooring not far away.

"Let's go, fellas," Bernie called to his crew. Like clockwork, the four scrambled.

Within minutes, the small Coast Guard boat approached the *36500*. It was almost totally dark. All they had to see with was a flashlight. They couldn't see much.

At that same moment, the telephone rang at the Nickerson home.

Mary Nickerson picked up the call on the first ring.

"Hello, this is Mary Nickerson," answered Jack's mother.

"Mary, it's Kathleen," replied George's mother. "I just wanted to call to say that George could not convince Jack to stay for supper even though he tried."

It took Mrs. Nickerson a few moments before a quiet panic set in.

"Why Kathleen, whatever do you mean? Isn't Jack still there at your house with George and Sinbad?"

"Why no, he left a few hours ago. He said he needed to do something, a chore or plan or something. At least that's what George said," answered Mrs. Sears.

There was quiet on the line. Now it was Mrs. Sears's turn to be worried.

"Is Jack not at home?"

"No, he's not. I thought he was with you. Listen, Kathleen, I have to go now. Something about this just doesn't feel right. Call it a mother's instinct. It's dark and there's no sign of Jack. I'll phone you when he turns up. He probably went into town to find Joshua. You know how these younger brothers like to tag along with their older ones!"

"Okay, Mary, sure. But don't forget to call. This has gotten me worried."

As soon as Kathleen hung up, Jack's mother put down the phone. Her mind was in a thousand places trying to piece together where Jack might have gone.

Susannah started to fuss; it was time for her supper. As Mrs. Nickerson put Susannah in her high chair, the kitchen door opened. Thinking it was Jack, Mrs. Nickerson turned around quickly to remind her youngest son to explain himself. But Jack wasn't there. Instead, Sam Nickerson and Joshua came through the door, knocking snow off their boots in the mudroom and taking off their coats, hats and gloves.

Mr. Nickerson noticed the worried look on his wife's face.

"Dear, what's wrong?" Sam asked his wife.

"Isn't Jack with you?" she asked, although she already knew the answer.

"Joshua," Mrs. Nickerson turned toward her eldest child, "did you see your brother today?"

"No, Mom, I was shoveling all day, and Dad just came into town to pick me up. We didn't see Jack at all."

"Oh, no, then I don't know where he is," she said, almost in a whisper.

"Our boy is missing," Mary then said to her husband.

Mrs. Nickerson explained to her husband and Joshua that Jack had gone to George's and was expected to stay there through dinner. But she had just received a call from Kathleen Sears, who said that Jack had left two hours earlier.

"We have to start searching for him!" Mrs. Nickerson said.

"Son, put your coat back on," Mr. Nickerson replied. "We are going back out." Joshua did as his father asked. He, too, was worried about his brother.

"Where will you go first?" asked Jack's mother.

"We'll make the rounds around town," Sam said. "We'll start first on Main Street, then swing by

the Coast Guard station, check in with the harbormaster and then go on from there," he added. "But first I'll alert the police department to be on the lookout. Josh, go warm up the truck and I'll be out in a minute."

From a corner in the kitchen, Granny Eldredge heard everything as she sat next to the short-wave radio. She lowered her head in deep worry.

Susannah continued to cry for her supper.

CHAPTER 8

IS JACK SAFE?

It was Bernie who noticed the dory tied to the *36500*. Even in the near-darkness, a boat tied to another boat is an easy thing to see.

"Hey, Andy, Ervin and Richard," Bernie called to his crew as they readied the boat to take off, "stop what you're doing and come to the wheelhouse. Look at that dory tied to the *36500*."

Bernie turned on the *36500* engine, and it climbed to life quickly. The engine rumbled and the boat came alive, idling at the ready, as if awaiting its orders.

As the three crewmen walked toward Bernie, they, too, saw the small dory bobbing up and down next to the *36500*. Andy turned on the spotlight for a better look. Bernie's heart sank. Inside the dory were a child's boot and a red wool blanket. Thanks to the spotlight, the red blanket shone like a Christmas light.

With a knowing and sinking feeling in his soul, Bernie began thinking the worst. Experience had told him that hope was a luxury in these cases.

"That sure looks like Sam Nickerson's dory," Bernie said. And the initials JEN were clearly visible on the blanket. Bernie stooped down to pick it up and held it in his hands. He also grabbed Jack's boot.

"Oh no, oh no," shouted Bernie, who had just confirmed it was indeed the Nickerson dory. "Hey guys, that's Sam Nickerson's dory, and I think young Jack was on it."

"Do you think Jack rowed that dory out here himself?" asked Richard. "Could he have fallen *overboard*?" All four of the Coast Guardsmen were wide-eyed with worry about Jack, not to mention the rescue mission they were about to leave on.

Andy immediately directed the spotlight to the waterline in an attempt to find Jack. Andy made several passes back and forth, but there was no sign of the boy.

Ervin said to Bernie, "There's no way that kid could have survived the cold, even for a few minutes."

Bernie's heart sank. What if Jack had died? Bernie took in a deep breath. Here he was about to set off on a rescue mission in a hurricane when his young friend was probably dead.

"Andy, is the radio fired up? I need to call this into the harbormaster and the station. They can alert Jack's family."

Just as Bernie reached out to grab the two-way radio, Bernie, Andy, Ervin and Richard heard a sound sneak through the roar of the nor'easter.

A low, gruff barking of a dog.

And it was coming from the survivor compartment just feet away from them.

Bernie threw open the door and was greeted with a giant lick of a dog's tongue.

Ervin and Richard's flashlight illuminated the giant yellow dog with its wagging tail. And next to him, the figure of ten-year-old

Jack Nickerson curled up on a pallet of wool blankets, sleeping. Sinbad had been keeping him warm.

Jack was missing a boot, but he was alive and warm and apparently very tired!

Bernie and his crew breathed a sigh of relief. Bernie muttered a prayer of thanks that Jack was safe and alive.

"Andy, do me a favor," Bernie said. "Get on the horn and get someone from the station over to the Nickerson place and tell his family to meet us at the fish pier. We will pull up alongside the pier and drop off Jack and Sinbad. Better alert the police department and harbormaster's office, too, in case Sam Nickerson has already sent the word out to find his boy."

"Right away, Bernie."

As Andy was relaying the messages, Bernie gently tapped Jack on the shoulder.

"Jack, hey, wake up, buddy."

In an instant, Jack was awake and frightened. His hazel eyes opened wide. It took a moment for Jack to remember where he was. When he saw Bernie, he jumped into his arms. "Geez, am I glad to see you!"

Then Jack told Bernie what had happened as Bernie's crew made the short detour to the

fish pier to wait for Jack's father to come and get him. Bernie listened intently, wrapping Jack's red blanket around him.

As luck would have it, Bernie thought, there were more wool blankets the Coast Guard had placed inside the survivor's cabin for a future mission. This was too good to be true! Especially since Jack had already lost a boot and the blanket Granny had given him. Jack had been wearing wool socks, so at least there was something on his feet, but his foot was cold.

Jack told Bernie he had made a pallet of wool blankets on the floor of the cabin. His stomach was getting queasy from the boat bobbing up and down in the waves. Sinbad didn't look so great either. The yellow lab now lay on his side on the pile of blankets, whimpering every so often, but his eyes were still alert.

Jack had snuggled in beside Sinbad. He thought that even if he wanted to, he probably couldn't get back in the dory and row to shore; it was too dangerous in the dark. All he could do was wait for Bernie. Scared, Jack worried that Bernie wasn't coming and that he and Sinbad would have to spend the night alone aboard the *36500*, that maybe Bernie and his crew had taken another boat to rescue the *Pendleton* crew.

Jack had closed his eyes and thrown his arms around Sinbad's neck. The dog put his head on Jack's leg, and Jack closed his eyes. At that point Jack, exhausted, must have fallen asleep. But Sinbad made sure he was extra warm.

After Jack had slipped and lost his boot, he told Bernie, he had managed to scamper aboard the *36500*. He and Sinbad made their way to the survivors' cabin. It was unlocked! They dove inside, away from the nor'easter.

What saved Jack's life, Bernie and his crew realized, was that someone had left the survival compartment unlocked the last time the *36500* was used, and Jack had remembered to try to get in there. Luckily, the boy was alive to tell his story.

It was cold inside the survival cabin, and there was hardly any daylight. But at least Jack and Sinbad were out of the wind. Sinbad's giant, warm body, the extra blankets stored in the survivors' compartment, Jack's wool coat and shelter from the wind, all were on Jack's side.

As he told his story to Bernie, a tear rolled down Jack's freckled cheek.

"I'm so sorry, Bernie! Look at the trouble I caused. My mom and dad are going to kill me."

Turning his face away so he wouldn't laugh, Bernie tried to be serious: "Don't worry about it, kid, I'm just glad you're alive."

"Hey, Bernie," Andy called out, "I reached Chatham P-D and left a message that Jack was okay. And better yet, Chatham P-D had just gotten a visit from Jack's dad, who was at headquarters when I was on the horn with them, so Mr. Nickerson's going to meet us at the pier in a few minutes to pick up Jack and Sinbad."

"Leave the dory tied to our stern and we'll tow it in," ordered Bernie. "Hey Andy," Bernie said to the junior engineman, "thank you!"

"No problem!"

Bernie bundled Jack up tight as a drum. He buttoned his coat as Jack struggled not to yawn. "You had me very worried, my little friend," Bernie said to Jack as he made sure his gloves were on. Bernie also put Jack's boot back on and double-tied his lace. "There's no way this boot will come off now!" Bernie explained.

Jack and Sinbad stayed behind Bernie as the coxswain steered the *36500* toward the fish pier about twenty yards away. Already they could see two pairs of headlights: one from Sam Nickerson's truck and the other from a Chatham Police Department squad car.

As the boat pulled alongside the pier and Sam Nickerson ran down the walkway toward his son, Jack remembered something he had for Bernie.

The boy pulled a white cotton napkin from his coat pocket.

"Here, Bernie," said Jack, handing the small mound to Bernie. "I saved you a Cushman's donut in case you got real hungry."

"Ah, geez, kid, you didn't have to do that, but I promise you I'll eat it, and thank you!"

"Bernie, may I ask you a question?"

"Sure, kid, anything."

"Do you promise you'll come back, that nothing will happen to you, okay?"

For a moment Bernie said nothing to Jack.

"Jack, I promise you I'll try my very best," said Bernie. "And it's a promise I intend to keep."

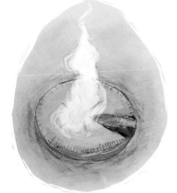

CHAPTER 9

THE DARING RESCUE

J ack Nickerson was at his mother's kitchen table faster than a cottontail rabbit can hop across a meadow by the time Bernie, Andy, Ervin and Richard had crossed the Chatham Bar in search of the crew of the *Pendleton.*

Minutes before, on the short ride from the pier to home, Jack had sat between his father and his treasured older brother, Joshua, who protectively put his arm around Jack's shoulder. Jack's head lay on Joshua's arm.

When they walked into the warm, cozy kitchen, Mary Nickerson let out a cry of joy and ran toward her middle child.

She wiped the snow from atop Jack's head as Granny Eldredge took off his boots. "Whoever tied this one lace knotted it tighter than a barrel full of mackerel," she observed.

Jack just smiled.

A feast of chicken potpie topped with homemade buttermilk biscuits was laid on the table for the Nickerson men. Baby Susannah, Granny Lucille and Mary had already eaten as they waited with worried hearts for Jack's safe return.

The police department had phoned Mrs. Nickerson at Sam's request to let her know that Jack was safe and on his way home. It was then that Mrs. Nickerson called her cousin, Kathleen Sears, to let George's mother know that Jack was safe.

There would be plenty of time, Sam Nickerson thought to himself, for him and Jack to have a long conversation about the wisdom of taking a dory out in the hurricane. It was enough simply to have his youngest son safe. Sam Nickerson guessed his wife was thinking the very same thing.

As Mrs. Nickerson cleared away the supper dishes, Granny Eldredge turned up the short-wave radio. They could hear all kinds of chatter coming from the radio that carried Coast Guard transmissions about the rescue. For a moment, no one moved or spoke. All ears were on the radio, listening intently.

From what Granny Eldredge could pick up, and as she explained to her family, Bernie had miraculously cleared the treacherous Chatham Bar. Sometimes the bar was so shallow that boats had problems pushing on through. But Bernie was an expert and always said he had full faith in the *36500*.

While the family waited for more news, Mary Nickerson placed a hot apple pie on the table.

"My favorite!" said Jack.

"Is there vanilla ice cream too, Ma?" asked Joshua.

"Oh, *pie!*" shouted Susannah, and everyone around the table laughed.

Sam and Mary Nickerson knew their son well enough to know that the normal bedtime would not apply tonight. There was no way to unglue Jack from the kitchen table where he sat with Granny Eldredge and Joshua listening to the short-wave radio. Sinbad slept on the floor on a rug at Jack's feet.

"What's happening now, Granny?" asked Joshua.

"Well, dear, there's chatter that Bernie and the *36500* crew have found the *Pendleton*! The stern of the ship is about five miles northwest of Chatham. But it's in very bad shape. The ship has snapped in two, right in half, because of the strong waves and winds," she explained. "Apparently the bow floated away hours ago, and thirty-three survivors are in the stern section. That's all I know for now."

"Wow, that must be an incredible sight!" Jack imagined.

"Considering it is pitch-dark, dear, I'm not sure if there's much to see. Let's continue to listen, shall we? I'm sure you'll always remember this evening."

"Oh, for sure!"

Jack's parents listened to this exchange between grandmother and grandson with amusement—and relief. Their son could easily have been killed tonight, and they were grateful Jack was alive and well. Same thing for Sinbad.

It was a miracle this had happened. While Granny kept her grandsons occupied, the Nickerson phone kept ringing. Everyone, it seemed, in the town of Chatham had heard about Jack's mad dash in the dory and was calling to see how he was. This was out of neighborly concern, not nosiness.

A few men on the police force had told their wives, who told their friends and husbands, and pretty soon everyone had a stake in Jack's welfare. Jack's parents took turns answering the calls.

Everyone had also heard about the *Pendleton* and was anxious to know if Bernie and his crew would survive and save the men aboard the *Pendleton*'s stern section. There was another vessel in distress: earlier in the day the *Fort Mercer* had also snapped in two. This had happened north of the *Pendleton* and farther offshore. Even though the *Pendleton* had broken apart closer to Provincetown, the stern of the vessel had floated toward Chatham.

Both vessels were caught in the storm. They were from the southern states, heading north with their cargoes of kerosene heating oil. Each ship was just over five hundred feet in length, longer than a football field. The way the cargoes were spaced made it easy for the strong waves and winds to tear apart the ships.

The Coast Guard and the Navy were helping with that separate rescue effort. No doubt about it, February 18, 1952, was going to be a huge day to remember in Coast Guard history.

Jack overheard the phone conversations people were having with his parents.

"Mom and Dad, I have a great idea!" Jack chipped in, adding, "Anytime folks call the house, tell them to listen to the short-wave, and the minute Bernie is on his way in, let's all meet at the fish pier with blankets and cars and trucks to help the survivors off, and we'll help drive everyone to the Coast Guard station." Jack was remembering how the wool blankets inside the survivors' compartment had kept him warm.

"Son, that's a thoughtful and considerate idea," Sam commented. "I'll pass the word around. There's a town meeting tonight, so I'll call a few folks who are going to share news of the plan."

And so he did.

CHAPTER 10

JACK'S PLAN

The network in a small New England town is tight, and people passed on "Jack's Plan" to their friends and neighbors. Because Chatham was a sea town at the elbow of Cape Cod, with family working the water in the fishing trade and other maritime occupations, many families had short-wave radios. Nearly everyone had a telephone. So passing news around was wicked easy.

If Bernie and his crew lived, if Andy, Richard, Ervin and Bernie survived the nor'easter and rescued the crew, everyone would know about it and know when it was time to get to the pier to help. "Granny, what's happening now?" Jack asked.

"He did it!" Granny Eldredge shared. "He's got thirty-two merchant mariners off the *Pendleton*. Now I just heard on the radio that he's on his way in. Another Coast Guard vessel, however, wanted Bernie to bring the survivors to their ship and do an at-sea transfer, but I can't imagine that will work."

"I'll bet Bernie didn't like hearing that!" Jack said.

"Apparently he didn't," Granny added, "because it sounds like he just turned off his radio!"

Joshua was just as interested in the mission as Jack. "I wonder what will happen next?" he wondered.

"That's something I'm sure the whole town is asking right about this moment," imagined Granny.

"But I thought there were thirty-three survivors aboard?" asked Joshua.

"Son, something might have happened," answered Samuel, adding, "We will have to wait and see."

For a long while there was no word from Bernie or the *36500*. The radio was silent except for the Motor Lifeboat Station and a Coast Guard cutter trying to reach Bernie and his crew.

"Charlie Golf Three Six Five Hundred, this is Chatham Station, over." There was no response.

The crew at the Chatham Motor Life Boat Station sat in the control room, waiting.

The Nickerson family sat at the kitchen table, waiting.

The whole town of Chatham stopped what they were doing, waiting for word.

Then it came: "Chatham Station, this is Charlie Golf Three Six Five Hundred, inbound Chatham entrance lighted buoy with thirty-six souls on board."

Bernie had turned his radio back on! Jack heard the voice of his dear friend thunder over the short-wave radio. Bernie had found his way back! He was alive, and so were Andy, Ervin and Richard. Bernie's transmission said he was rounding Morris Island and heading up to the harbor. Bernie asked that ambulances be at the ready and requested "help down at the pier for the survivors."

In fact, Bernie was heading toward the channel between Aunt Lydia's Cove and the fish pier. Many years later, he would remember that the pier was "jam-packed" with people. The transmission indicated Bernie had, by chance, found the red lighted buoy marking the entrance to Chatham Harbor in the storm.

Soon the *36500* would be at the fish pier.

Everyone in Chatham sprang into action. All over town, thanks to Jack's idea, people grabbed blankets from storage chests and even tore blankets from their beds to wrap survivors with once the *36500* reached the pier.

"Dad, we gotta go!" Jack shouted, clutching his red blanket. "Please!" Jack intended the blanket for only one person: Bernie.

"Son, I'm two steps ahead of you," replied Sam Nickerson, who was already putting on his coat. "Joshua, aren't you coming too?"

"Dad, I wouldn't miss this for anything," said Joshua. "Let's go."

"I'm coming too!" said Mary Nickerson. "And I just talked to Kathleen and George and they're bringing George Jr. We couldn't let you boys not share this with us."

Granny Eldredge offered to stay at the house while Susannah slept; the baby was far too young to be out in a hurricane. And Granny felt too old to want to leave the warmth of the house. "Just come back and tell me all about it!" she requested.

While the boys, Sam and Mary were bundled up in their winter gear, Granny pulled together some spare blankets to wrap around the survivors.

And they were off just as the short wave announced that the *36500* had cleared the entrance to Chatham Harbor.

"Dad, we gotta *hurry!*" Jack urged.

CHAPTER 11

THE PROMISE KEPT

The storm was beginning to quiet, like a child firmly and properly disciplined. The worst of the nor'easter may have died down, but the weather was still nasty. Bitter cold lay over the Lower Cape where Chatham met the sea.

That didn't stop the hardy folks who lived there. A stream of headlights swam along Main Street like herring heading upstream, bound for the fish pier: station wagons, pickup trucks and cars, whatever people had in their yards. The Coast Guard had its handful of vehicles to ferry survivors and was proud that its Chatham neighbors were picking up the slack.

Then the running lights of the *36500* appeared in the distance. For a moment no one said a word, even though there were close to one hundred people crowding in on the pier. Closer the motor lifeboat came until the outlines of many people could be seen. As Coxswain Bernie expertly guided the *36500* alongside the pier, the crowd erupted in support, clapping and cheering to welcome the rescuers and the rescued home.

Jack saw that Bernie was clearly exhausted, and Jack's fingers gripped his red blanket in both worry and excitement. George and Joshua, too, were caught up in the crowd's excitement.

As soon as the lines were secured, Andy, Richard and Ervin began helping the survivors from the boat deck to the pier into the waiting arms of the people of Chatham. Bernie remained behind the wheel and began powering down *36500*'s single ninety-horsepower engine.

One by one, each of the *Pendleton* crewmen had a blanket or two wrapped around his shoulders and was hurried into a waiting vehicle. Every seaman rescued was frightened, exhausted, cold, wet and hungry. All had lost most every personal item aboard the *Pendleton*—family pictures, watches, articles of clothing. They had nothing but what they wore and some cash from a poker game.

Still, their grateful eyes shone through to everyone in the crowd, and they seemed to bow their heads in grateful acknowledgment for the brave men in the Coast Guard who had saved their lives.

Within minutes the crowd began to disperse. Bernie was still on the boat, as was Andy, seeing that the *36500* was secured. One of the last survivors to disembark was eighteen-year-old Charlie Bridges, a soft-spoken southerner who came up to Bernie and simply said two words: "Thank you."

"You're quite welcome," Bernie replied. At that moment, someone tugged on Charlie's shoulder, threw a blanket around his shoulders and said, "Let's get you warm at the station, young man." Charlie quietly followed.

"Mr. Webber, you and your crew were certainly inspiring," said Charlie over his shoulder. "I'll never forget that you saved my life."

For the first time in hours, Bernie deeply exhaled. He rested his right arm on the wheel of the *36500* and stared out into the night with Ervin nearby. It would be years before any of the *36500* crew could begin to articulate their shared experience.

Not mature enough to know when he was intruding, or too young to care, Jack approached Bernie. He didn't say a word; perhaps he knew the value of silence. Bernie must have heard Jack's boots crunching through the snow and turned toward him. Bernie was relieved to see Jack.

The friends smiled at each other, their bond strong enough to speak without using words. It didn't matter that their ages were years apart, for true friendship does not measure in years.

"Hey kid, glad to see ya," said Bernie.

Jack couldn't speak because the lump in his throat was too large. Tears stung beneath his eyes, but this time, Jack cried for joy and not out of fear. The Nickerson lad jumped at Bernie, threw his arms around Webber's neck and stayed there. Bernie held him close and, after a moment, put Jack down. Bernie felt something warm around his neck.

"You can borrow my blanket to keep yourself warm," Jack said.

"Thank you, I promise I'll return it," Bernie said.

"You've already kept your promise," Jack explained. "You're back, safe and sound, and think of all the people you saved."

CHAPTER 12

THE MISSION IS OVER

I t was a team effort," Bernie said, adding, "I couldn't have done what I did without Andy, Ervin and Richard."

Sam Nickerson and Joshua approached Bernie. Sam held out his hand. "It's an honor to know you, Bernie, and to call you my friend." Bernie returned the firm grip.

"Now let's get you back to the station along with anyone else who needs a lift," Sam offered. "My friend George Sears is waiting, and he's got extra room." George Sears gave Andy and Ervin a ride back to the Chatham Motor Life Boat Station. Richard had gone ahead in another vehicle.

Bernie rode in the front passenger seat of Sam Nickerson's truck, with Mrs. Nickerson, Joshua and Jack in the back. Jack's blanket was still snug around Bernie's shoulders. As much as Jack had wanted to bring him, Mrs. Nickerson forbade Sinbad from coming that night. She felt he might be a bother to everyone at the Coast Guard station. Sinbad didn't seem to mind; he was curled up in front of the stove back home.

Within minutes, Sam Nickerson's pickup pulled into the crowded parking lot at the Coast Guard station. An exhausted Bernie got out and walked inside with the Nickersons. The Searses dropped off their passengers and also gave Mrs. Nickerson a ride home. "I've got to tell Granny all about it!" Mary gushed.

Inside, chaos reigned triumphant. To Jack, the station seemed a magical place. There was sound and laughter and joy and relief everywhere. He had never seen so many men cry so openly before.

The mighty radiator even hissed its support with the gurgling sound of hot water in the pipes. A tea kettle sung its readiness in the galley. The smell of hot chicken soup washed over everyone's heads. The short-wave radio cackled with numerous calls. Phones were ringing off the hook. Wet clothing lay on the floor, discarded by the *Pendleton* crew. Instead, they were loaned Coast Guard clothing until theirs had dried out. Richard C. Kelsey, a renowned local photographer, snapped pictures that would, in the years ahead, become an important part of the record of that rescue mission and its aftermath.

Pendleton survivors were sitting, standing and lying around the room everywhere. Around them all, people gathered. Dr. Carroll Keene was taking care of them. The Reverend Steve Smith was there, too, in case spiritual help was necessary.

"Hey, Dad, isn't that...?"

Sam said, "That's right, Jack. That's Mr. Ben Shufro of Puritan Clothing, measuring the men for new clothing."

Jack had seen Mr. Shufro sometimes on Main Street, where Puritan Clothing was located. Jack had always waved to him. Puritan would donate a lot of clothing to the men that night.

Jack looked at Bernie, who was quiet. He seemed to be taking in all the fuss but at the

same time held back, too. "Jack, I'll be back in a minute," Bernie said. "I have to check on Andy, Richard and Ervin."

Bernie needn't have worried. The trio was at a nearby table being interviewed by local radio legend Ed Semprini. Bernie would soon be interviewed by Ed as well.

In between the many excited voices, laughter and crying, Jack overheard several survivors describe their harrowing experience and his friend Bernie's heroism. One *Pendleton* crewman who didn't appear much older than Jack told how the big ship had put over a thirty-five-foot-long Jacob's ladder so they could climb down the side of the ship to be rescued by the four men in the *36500*. The young man described how he was given the ride of his life as he climbed down the long ladder. He described how the ladder swayed out from the ship in a wide arc as the ship rolled to starboard and then how he and his shipmates were thrown back hard against the steel side of the *Pendleton* when the ship rolled back to port.

Another *Pendleton* survivor spoke of how the men in the bow of the *36500* had saved him when he had fallen off the ladder after he had been slammed against the side of the big ship by a huge sixty-foot wave. This man spoke of the courage of Bernie's crew and how all of them risked their lives.

Yet another survivor spoke about the crowded conditions on the small rescue boat. The man, a seasoned mariner, knew the *36500* was badly overloaded and unstable, but he was both happy and incredibly scared when he was stuffed in the small engine room with other survivors and the small boat's engineer. Here, he saw engineer Andy Fitzgerald fighting to keep the small, ninety-horsepower engine going as the waves rolled the small boat so far over that the engine lost its prime and occasionally stalled.

One of the first men to be rescued by Bernie and his crew told of how many times the small boat was almost crushed by the larger ship when rescuing *Pendleton* survivors. Bernie had to sometimes go underneath the big ship by the huge propeller when some men fell off the ladder or drifted away from their rescuers. This man also described the incredible seamanship demonstrated by Bernie as he had to guide the *36500* down huge sixty-foot waves that pushed the small boat forward very fast and then had to reverse the engine forcefully so as not to crash into the *Pendleton*.

This same man stood by Bernie the whole time and overheard him praying several times and watched the pain cross his face when one *Pendleton* sailor could not be saved. The man also watched as the last survivor came onboard just as the big ship groaned one last time and rolled over into its watery grave off Chatham.

Jack couldn't believe these stories. Some of the thirty-two men on the station's mess deck who were saved were so relieved to be rescued that they passed out and had to be revived with smelling salts by Dr. Keene. He overheard Dr. Keene explain that the men's nervous systems were so overtaxed with the adrenalin of their near-death experience that they passed out when they finally accepted they were safe.

Bernie did reach a phone to call his wife, Miriam. "I can only talk a few minutes," he told the young Mrs. Webber. "I'm fine and I'll be in touch with you tomorrow." The Nickersons were still hanging around with their friends and neighbors, helping where they could, when Bernie found them again in the crowded station.

"We're heading out," said Sam. "Don't see the need to stay since you all have it under control. Again, I'm so happy you made it out of that storm alive!"

"Same here, Sam. And I'm glad your dory wasn't lost, either, let alone your son!"

"Jack," said Bernie, turning toward the youngest Nickerson, "thank you again for the loan of your blanket. I'll return it soon, I promise. And one other thing: I ate the Cushman's donut you saved for me minutes after I dropped you off at the pier. Thanks, buddy!"

And with that, Bernie disappeared into the crowd at the station.

Sam Nickerson took his boys home.

That night Bernie slept well, resting his head on Jack's red blanket. When he woke up the next morning, he was covered in dollar bills. As a sign of thanks and gratitude, the merchant seamen he rescued off the *Pendleton* had showered him with their last dollars, and he awoke in a sea of green the next morning.

True to his character, instead of keeping the money for himself, Bernie gave the money to the officer in charge, who used it to buy the station's first television set.

Young Jack Nickerson slept soundly that night as well. His friend Bernie was safe, as were Andy, Richard and Ervin and the men aboard the *Pendleton*.

As he nodded off, with Sinbad on the floor nearby, Jack dreamed of a career in the Coast Guard.

CHAPTER 13

MAY 15, 2002

The day opened with bright skies the color of sapphires, utterly sun-drenched and beautiful. But it was cold outside, at least in the forties, making it feel like a day in March. The Coast Guard had planned a very special day for May 15, 2002, at Coast Guard Station Chatham. The previous day had been the fiftieth-anniversary reunion of the *36500* crew who had rescued thirty-two crewmen from the sinking *Pendleton* off Chatham on February 18, 1952.

Fifty years earlier, in 1952, Bernie Webber, Andy Fitzgerald, Ervin Maske and Richard

Livesey left the Chatham Motor Life Boat Station. In the spring of 1952, each of the four men was awarded the Coast Guard's highest honor, the Gold Lifesaving Medal. And today, all four were at the reunion with their families. It was a day to be treasured forever.

It would also be a wonderful reunion between old friends Bernie and Jack. How much each man's life had changed since the day the pair became friends over fifty years before!

The day began with a ride aboard the *36500* for Bernie, Ervin, Andy and Richard. They were accompanied by two Coast Guardsmen, Master Chief John E. "Jack" Downey and Senior Chief Sheila Lucey, then officer in charge of Coast Guard Station Brant Point on Nantucket. At one point Bernie took the tiller. He said "it seemed perfectly normal" to be driving the boat, even after fifty years. The six had a great time on the water.

Then it was off to the Coast Guard station, where a luncheon was served in the very room where Bernie and his crew had scrounged for donuts on that frigid night fifty years before.

The Town of Chatham kicked in for a large cake. There were speeches aplenty. Carole Maloof, a Chatham favorite, sang the national anthem. As the youngest of the four Gold Medal honorees, Andy Fitzgerald was given the "duty" of unveiling a bronze plaque in honor of his crewmates. Selectmen Douglas Ann Bohman and Parker Wiseman represented the Town of Chatham. The First Coast Guard District chaplain, Naval Lieutenant Commander T.A. Yuille, delivered the invocation. And Captain James Murray, commander of Group Woods Hole, which oversaw the Chatham station, said a few words as well.

It was a big day for Coast Guard Station Chatham. Senior Chief Steve Lutjen did a wonderful job hosting. Other local folks served on the Reunion Planning Committee, including Bob and Donna Weber (who were no relation to Bernie), Stanley and Bonnie Snow, Dick Ryder, Donnie St. Pierre and Bill Quinn.

Jack loved being an invited guest, hearing all the speeches and catching up with old friends. Even seeing the station's mascot, a chocolate Labrador named Zoe, reminded Jack of his beloved Sinbad so many years ago.

Through the years, Bernie Webber and Jack had stayed in touch. The pair remained fast friends despite their age difference. Bernie was that friendly uncle to Jack.

Not long after the 1952 rescue, Bernie was transferred from the Chatham Motor Life Boat Station. He would return in the years ahead as officer in charge. The Nickersons continued to see Bernie and his growing family.

When Bernie retired from the Coast Guard in 1966, the Nickersons were invited to his celebration, including Jack, then twenty-four. Jack was the same age Bernie had been back in 1952 at the time of the big rescue.

By this time, Jack was in the Coast Guard. He went through basic training at Curtis Bay, Maryland, before being transferred to duty in District One, which included his beloved home waters of Cape Cod.

Jack had pretty much started out like Bernie, a humble seaman, and worked very hard to eventually become a rated bosun's mate. He rose through the ranks as an accomplished mariner, using the skills he and his dad had honed in the *Susannah*, and exhibited a strength of character learned from observing Bernie and his friends during his early childhood.

Later in his career, he had been fast-tracked for promotion and given the toughest assignments and eventually command of his own rescue station and command of a coastal cutter. He and his crews were always recognized for their readiness and capabilities. Jack had joined the Coast Guard after graduation from the Massachusetts Maritime Academy and was close to retiring as a chief warrant officer in 2002 after almost forty years of distinguished service.

Throughout the day, as Jack waited patiently to see Bernie, Bernie saw many people he knew from his Coast Guard days. He was becoming tired very fast. The festivities that had stretched over several days had worn him out. At seventy-four, he was still a vigorous, strong man. His emotions, however, were another story! So many memories with which to deal; memories of lives rescued and lives lost. There were so many people surrounding Bernie that he had trouble finding someone in the crowd whom he had wanted to see badly. It was an overwhelming day.

Where was Jack? Bernie wondered.

CHAPTER 14

BEST FRIENDS FOREVER

S everal people told Bernie that Jack
was at the station too, so Bernie knew
it was only a matter of time before the
pair met up.

Jack had been tucked into quiet corners
during all the fuss at the station. He saw
Bernie from a distance. He even tried once or
twice to approach his old friend. But he had
no luck there because so many people were
around Bernie.

Finally, though, Chief Warrant Officer
Nickerson saw Retired Chief Warrant Officer
Webber at the same time.

The two friends approached each other in the same room where fifty years earlier Jack gave Bernie his bedside blanket to keep him warm. It seemed that so much had changed, yet here they were, with a friendship that was untarnished. Where Cushman donuts had been traded and eaten. Where the old radiator hissed in the aftermath of the successful mission. Where the short-wave radio echoed with the excitement of both the danger and daring of that night.

"And there he is, young Jack Nickerson!" said Bernie, extending his arms for a giant bear hug for his friend.

The two men embraced.

Both Jack and Bernie were glad that they had not lost touch through the years.

It was Bernie who occasionally fished with Joshua, Jack and Sam Nickerson on the *Susannah* on a Sunday afternoon. Then he and Miriam would join the family for supper. It was Bernie who acted as an advisor to Jack when Jack wrote a high school paper on the Coast Guard. And it was Bernie, then stationed in Woods Hole in the early 1960s, whom Jack called when Sinbad didn't wake up one morning.

"Will you help me bury him?"

"I'm on my way to Chatham," was all Bernie needed or had to say.

Even though Jack was a young man by the time Sinbad died, he still relied on his friend in troubling times.

And Bernie relied on Jack, too. Helping him and Miriam move. Helping Bernie paint a boat and all kinds of things.

This is how it was between Jack and Bernie. Always there for each other, in good times and in times of grief and sadness.

"Tell me how you've been," asked Bernie. "How is your family? I haven't had a chance to stop by the Nickerson house, and I've been wondering. It's been several years since I've seen your father."

"Dad wasn't feeling too well, so he said he'll catch up with you when you stop by the house later," explained Jack. "And Joshua and his family will be joining us too. Susannah lives in Boston, but she sends her best."

"I'm sorry about your mother's passing," said Bernie. "I'll always remember Mary as a wonderful wife and mother."

"Thank you, Bernie," Jack said quietly, "we miss her every day."

The pair exchanged notes further on family. Bernie's daughter, Pattie Hamilton, and her husband, Bruce, and their daughters, Hilary and Leah, were at the reunion. So was Miriam, who was a bride in 1952.

Jack's wife, Caroline, had stopped by the gathering earlier but had to leave to pick up their grandson, but she would be stopping back at the station with the boy. His name was John, after his grandfather. Everyone took to calling him Young Jack.

"In fact, here comes Young Jack now," Jack noted to Bernie.

"Caroline, it's lovely to see you again," Bernie said to Jack's wife.

"And you as well. We'll look forward to catching up with you and Miriam later, once all the fuss has died down," Jack's wife said.

"And here," Caroline noted, "is our grandson, Young Jack."

A boy around ten with hazel eyes and freckles splashed across his face marched up to Bernie and extended his hand in greeting.

"Very nice to meet you, Sir."

"I hear your name is Jack," Bernie said, slightly bending over to meet the boy's gaze. For a moment the years washed away, and

Bernie noticed how much the boy looked like Jack at that age, so many decades ago.

"Yes, Sir, my full name is John Bernard Eldredge Nickerson. I actually have *four* names, and that's so cool."

Bernie's throat tightened. He felt honored that his name was now part of the Nickerson family. Until this moment, he had not known that Jack's grandson also carried his own name. The bonds of friendship became even stronger.

"Our son, Samuel, is named for his grandfather," Caroline explained. "And Samuel had grown up hearing about the famous rescue, and how much Bernie meant to Jack, so we carried on the legacy of friendship to another generation."

"I am truly touched," said Bernie humbly.

Just then a large yellow Labrador ran up to the small group and lunged himself at Young Jack.

"And this," Young Jack explained to Bernie, "is my best friend in the whole world. His name is Sinbad."

AUTHORS' AFTERWORD

*T*he *Daring Coast Guard Rescue of the Pendleton Crew* is based on the true-life rescue of thirty-two merchant seamen from the stern section of the SS *Pendleton* during a nor'easter off Cape Cod on the evening of February 18, 1952. During the same storm and forty miles to the north, the *Fort Mercer*, an identical 503-foot tanker, also snapped in two off the coast of Massachusetts.

The *Pendleton* was en route from Baton Rouge, Louisiana, with a cargo of kerosene and heating oil, bound for Boston. The *Fort Mercer* was headed to Portland, Maine, with a cargo of kerosene when it snapped in two around 8:00 a.m. on February 18.

Eight *Pendleton* crewmen perished when the ship broke apart shortly before 6:00 a.m. A ninth died while being rescued by Bernie and his *36500* crewmen. All told, between the rescued seamen on *Fort Mercer* and *Pendleton*, seventy of eighty-four merchant seamen were rescued by the Coast Guard between February 18 and 19, 1952.

In the spring of 1952, Bernie Webber and his three crewmen, Andy Fitzgerald, Richard Livesey and Ervin Maske, all received the Coast Guard's highest distinction, the Gold Lifesaving Medal, for their extraordinary courage and bravery on the night of their rescue. (Today, only Andy Fitzgerald is still living. Charles Bridges, the last known survivor of the *Pendleton* crew, passed away in May 2013. Like Bernie, Ervin and Richard, Charlie was a friend and is sadly missed.) In May 2002, the Coast Guard held the first-ever reunion of the Gold Medal Lifesaving Crew in Boston and on Cape Cod to commemorate the fiftieth anniversary of the famous rescue. In 2007, the Coast Guard issued its Top 10 Greatest Rescues of All Time and honored Webber and his crew, singling out the *Pendleton* rescue as its most significant small boat rescue since the service's inception in 1790.

Jack Nickerson and his family are fictionalized characters immersed throughout this book. George Sears, Jack's friend, and his family were also works of fiction. We felt, however, that Bernie should bond with a local child to make the story believable as a book for children. We are grateful to Richard Ryder for his remembrances of a childhood in Chatham that greatly inspired the character of Jack.

We tried our best to keep much of the rest of the story true and its timeline intact. The people mentioned who gathered at the Chatham Coast Guard Motor Life Boat Station (as it was known then) were real people.

We wrote this book to capture the magic, wonder, innocence and boyhood excitement of childhood in Chatham, circa 1952. We like to think Bernie would have appreciated our efforts.

FURTHER READING

To learn more about the Coast Guard's rescue mission of the *Pendleton* crew, readers are invited to the Coast Guard historian's website: www.uscg.mil/history/articles/pendleton_webster.asp.

Those interested in a longer, more detailed current version can purchase the authors' book *The* Pendleton *Disaster Off Cape Cod: The Greatest Small Boat Rescue in Coast Guard History* (Third Edition), www.amazon.com/Pendleton-Disaster-Off-Cape-Cod/dp/1609490509. The book is also available as an e-book.

Other characters in the story—such as Madaket Millie, one of the Coast Guard's and Nantucket's most storied volunteers, and Jack's dog, Sinbad—are real and were known to Bernie Webber. Readers interested in further researching Millie and Sinbad should consult the Coast Guard historian's website (see "Madaket Millie to the Rescue!" U.S. Naval Institute Proceedings 129 [August 2003] and www.uscg.mil/history/FAQS/FilmIndex.asp). Sinbad was featured in a 1946 film and a *New York Times* article chronicling his antics. We chose Sinbad as the name of Jack Nickerson's dog to honor the real Sinbad.

ABOUT THE AUTHORS

Journalist and historian Theresa M. Barbo is the author of six books of historical nonfiction published by The History Press. Her most recent work is *Cape Cod Wildlife: A History of Untamed Forests, Seas and Shores*, which examines the cultural relationship between humans and wildlife over the past four hundred years.

Barbo is also a noted public speaker in academic and professional circles and civic organizations throughout New England. She is a former executive in the nonprofit sector with a background in emergency communications, marine ecosystem conservation and wildlife animal and habitat protection.

A former award-winning broadcast journalist and newsmagazine history editor, Theresa holds a BA (English) and an MA (professional writing) from the University of Massachusetts–Dartmouth and certificates in executive integral leadership and supervisory development from the Mendoza College of Business at the University of Notre Dame. She has been recognized twice by the Coast Guard for her contributions to the preservation of the service's history.

Captain W. Russell Webster retired in 2003 after twenty-six years of Coast Guard service. He served as Group Woods Hole rescue commander from 1998 to 2001 and led his service's operational response to the John F. Kennedy Jr. and Egypt Air 990 crashes. He also served as the Coast Guard's regional operations officer for the September 11 terrorist attack responses.

After retirement, Webster continued his public service with the newly formed Transportation Security Administration at

Boston's Logan International Airport where he oversaw the daily security operations at eight federalized airports in Massachusetts. Webster co-led several regional transportation security planning efforts and played a key role in prototyping the TSA's earliest version of its passenger behavioral assessment program.

In 2008, he became FEMA's first New England federal preparedness coordinator responsible for coordinating preparedness activities in schools, businesses and communities. He has been recognized by the commandant of the Coast Guard, the Foundation for Coast Guard History and the First Coast Guard District commander for his efforts to further his service's proud heritage.

Together, Barbo and Webster, along with their colleague Master Chief John E. "Jack" Downey, co-founded Timeless Leadership Lessons of Yesteryear, an illustrated presentation that features the Top Ten Leadership Lessons from the *Pendleton* rescue mission. Since 2009, audiences at the following institutions and academies have heard them speak: Coast Guard Academy; the Leadership Development Center at the Coast Guard Academy; Norwich University;

Massachusetts Maritime Academy; Maine Maritime Academy; United States Merchant Marine Academy; SUNY Maritime, Bronx; and the Naval Academy Preparatory School in Newport.

Visit us at
www.historypress.net

....

This title is also available as an e-book